Jam & Honey

by **Melita Morales**

Illustrations by **Laura J. Bryant**

TRICYCLE PRESS
Berkeley

For my family—teaching me when
to hold still and when to spread my wings,
inspiring me with fearless exploration.
—M.M.

To Lynn
—L.B.

Text copyright © 2011 by Melita Morales
Illustrations copyright © 2011 by Laura Bryant

Published in the United States by Tricycle Press, an imprint of Random House Children's Books,
a division of Random House, Inc., New York.
www.randomhouse.com/kids

Tricycle Press and the Tricycle Press colophon are registered trademarks of Random House, Inc.

Library of Congress Cataloging-in-Publication Data

Morales, Melita.
  Jam and honey / by Melita Morales ; illustrations by Laura J. Bryant. — 1st ed.
      p. cm.
  Summary: Tells the story of a young girl and a honeybee who learn to coexist peacefully in the
same garden as they go about their respective tasks.
[1. Stories in rhyme. 2. Honeybee—Fiction. 3. Bees—Fiction.] I. Bryant, Laura J., ill. II. Title.
  PZ8.3.M7946Jam 2011
  [E]—dc22
                              2009041864

ISBN 978-1-58246-299-8 (hardcover)
ISBN 978-1-58246-390-2 (Gibraltar lib. bdg.)

Printed in China

Design by Betsy Stromberg

Typeset in Tarocco and Tyfa
The illustrations in this book were created with watercolors and pencil.

1 2 3 4 5 6 – 16 15 14 13 12 11

First Edition

The Girl

I'm going to pick berries,
all by myself,
enough to fill the bucket
high on the shelf.

When I come home
we'll make a treat,
sweet jam on toast
for me to eat.

The scratchy branches could scrape my knees,
but I'm more scared of the buzzing bees.

Mama says hold still, they will fly away.
Bees want nectar, so I'll be okay!

When I come home
we'll make a treat,
sweet jam on toast
for me to eat.

One for the bucket and one for me.
One for the bucket and one for —

OH!

It's a bee,
so loud and near,
but if I just stand still,
there's nothing to fear.

One for the bucket
and one for me.
Berries for the girl
and nectar for the bee.

When I come home
we'll make a treat,
sweet jam on toast
for me to eat.

The Bee

I'm going to get nectar, all on my own,
nectar from the vines where the flowers have grown.

We'll make honey when I come home,
sweet honey to fill our honeycomb.

Through scratchy branches I can duck and dive.
It's people that scare me when I leave the hive.

Mama says fly high, they will move away.
People want berries, so I'll be okay!

We'll make honey
when I come home,
sweet honey to fill
our honeycomb.

A drink for the hive tastes good to me.
A drink for the hive tastes good to —

OH!

It's a girl
and I feel scared,
but there are plenty of vines
for us to share.

A drink for the hive
tastes good to me.
Berries for the girl
and nectar for the bee.

We'll make honey
when I come home,
sweet honey to fill
our honeycomb.